PUFFIN BOOKS
Published by the Penguin Group
oks USA Inc., 375 Hudson Street, New York, New York 10014, U.S.A.
nguin Books Ltd, 27 Wrights Lane, London W8 5TZ, England
Penguin Books Australia Ltd, Ringwood, Victoria, Australia
oks Canada Ltd, 10 Alcorn Avenue, Toronto, Ontario, Canada M4V 3B2
Books (N.Z.) Ltd, 182-190 Wairau Road, Auckland 10, New Zealand

Books Ltd, Registered Offices: Harmondsworth, Middlesex, England

rst published in the United States of America by Lodestar Books,
an affiliate of E.P. Dutton, 1983
Published in Puffin Books, 1995

7 9 10 8

RARY OF CONGRESS HAS CATALOGED THE LODESTAR BOOKS EDITION AS FOLLOWS:
Wisler, G. Clifton.
Thunder on the Tennessee.
"Lodestar Books."
ry: Following his father's example, sixteen-year-old Willie Delamer joins the
d Texas Regiment and leaves his beloved Texas to fight for the Confederacy.
nited States—History—Civil War, 1861-1865—Fiction. 2. Texas—Fiction.]
I. Title.
PZ7.W78033Th 1983 [Fic] 82-21057 ISBN 0-525-67144-7

Puffin Books ISBN 0-14-037612-7

Printed in the United States of America

W9-BDC-221

THUN
ON T
TENNES

G. CLIFTON W

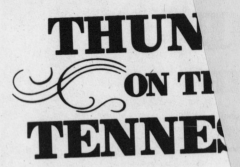

Penguin Bo
Pe

Penguin Bo
Penguin

Penguin

F

THE LIB

Summa
Secon
[1. U

Ex
it
c

PUFFIN BOOKS